Weekly Reader Children's Book Club presents

The Lion's Bed

Diane Redfield Massie

Publishing, Executive, and Editorial Offices:
Xerox Family Education Services
Middletown, Connecticut 06457

ISBN 0-88375-203-4

Library of Congress Catalogue Number

Weekly Reader Children's Book Club Edition
XEROX® is a trademark of Xerox Corporation.

For Timi

Hornbill loved his green-vine house in the top of the mango tree. "The jungle is peaceful here," said Hornbill, biting on a mango seed. "We all live together quietly, as friends should."

He waved to Anteater far below, busily collecting ants.

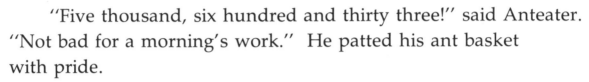

"Five thousand, six hundred and thirty three!" said Anteater.
"Not bad for a morning's work." He patted his ant basket
with pride.

"That's very good," said Hornbill.

Anteater smiled. "It's mangos for you, and ants for me!"
he said, twirling his ant basket, and he did a little dance
in the grass. "Oh, it's coconuts for monkeys, grass for elephants,
roots for peccaries, and ants for me!" sang Anteater. "Ants,
delicious ants for me!"

Hornbill stretched his wings and yawned.
"If we all ate the same thing . . . ."
"We'd be fighting and quarreling over
who was getting the most," said Anteater.
"Thank heavens no one else likes ants!"
He fastened the latch on his basket
and sat down to rest in the shade.

"You haven't mentioned me," said Python, looking down from the vine above him. "You haven't mentioned what *I* eat."

"Who knows what *you* eat?" said Anteater. "You're always asleep up there."

"Not always," said Python.

"Anyway, you don't eat ants, and that's all I care about," said Anteater.

Suddenly Elephant pushed his trunk through the vines.

"The peccaries are running through the grass," he said.
"They're very excited about something."

"They're always excited," said the monkeys. "Imagine being excited over roots!" They dropped their coconuts to the ground and hurried down to find them.

The peccaries came running under the trees. "THE LION'S COMING! THE LION'S COMING!" they cried, stumbling over the roots, and they fell in the grass.

"The LION?" said the monkeys.

"He's coming to live in *our* part of the jungle," said a peccary. "That's what the birds told us!"

"Let's hide!" cried the monkeys.

"Why is he coming *here*?" asked Hornbill. He flew down
and landed on a stone.

"Maybe there's more to eat over here," said Elephant.

"More of *us*," whimpered the monkeys.

"Or *us*!" squealed the peccaries, and they covered their eyes
with their hooves.

The monkeys were scrambling up in the trees.

Python closed his yellow-green eyes. "He won't bother *me*," he hissed.

"I'm beginning to wish," said Anteater, "that lions liked ants."

"Well, they don't," said Python. "They like anteaters."

"Heavens!" said Anteater. "I'm going to make my house stronger!"

"How?" asked Hornbill.

"With vines and grass and maybe some sticks!"

"That's not strong enough to keep lions out," called the monkeys. "You'll have to hide in the trees like us!"

"I can't climb trees," said Anteater.

"Neither can *we*!" cried the peccaries.

"Anyway," said Anteater, "you monkeys can't stay up there forever. How will you get the cracked coconuts in the grass?"

"Oh!" sighed the monkeys.
"We hadn't thought of that."

"Elephants are too big to hide,"
said Elephant. "What will I do?"
And he trumpeted loudly.

The monkeys were quarreling
among themselves, and the peccaries
began to cry.

"QUIET!" shouted Hornbill.
"WILL EVERYONE PLEASE BE QUIET!"

Everyone was quiet. Only the birds in the far-off trees were singing.

"Now," said Hornbill. "You should all be ashamed. You are thinking only of yourselves, and here we are all friends."

The monkeys came down to the lower branches and Python opened his eyes. The peccaries peeked out between the vines and Elephant sat down in the grass.

"What can we *do*?" asked Anteater.

"By ourselves we can't do much," said Hornbill, "but if we all work together, maybe we *can* do something."

"Let's have a meeting," said Anteater.

"Here!" said Elephant.

The peccaries came out from under the vines, and the monkeys jumped down behind them.

"First of all," said Hornbill, "we've got to decide what each of us is best at."

"I'm best with ants," said Anteater.

"We're best with coconuts," said the monkeys.

"I'm good at shaking things with my trunk," said Elephant.

"We're good at running," said the peccaries.

"And I'm best at singing,"
said Hornbill.

"Squawking," said Python.

"What are *you* best at?"
said Anteater. "Nothing!"

"That isn't true," said Python.
"I'm best at something,
but I won't say what it is."

"Who cares?" said Anteater.

"Please," said Hornbill. "We musn't quarrel. The lion will be here soon, and we've got to be ready." Hornbill hopped over next to the vines hanging from his mango tree. "We'll make a great big bed," he said, "right here under the vines."

"A BED?" said everyone. "What for?"

"For the lion, of course," said Hornbill.

"A BED FOR THE LION?"

"I'll explain in a minute," said Hornbill.
"Hurry!"

They hurried about, bringing grass and leaves, and they made a big, soft bed.

"Perfect!" said Hornbill.

"Are we making a bed so the lion can have a good
night's rest before he eats us all for breakfast?"
said Anteater.

"Who said anything about a rest?" said Hornbill,
and then he whispered his plan to his friends.

"We'll pick the coconuts!"
shouted the monkeys, and they
scampered off through
the trees.

"I'll bring the ants!"
said Anteater, and he hid with
his ant basket in the grass.
"We'll get ready to run!"
said the peccaries, and they
hid behind the vines.
"And I'll wait behind the mango
tree," said Elephant, "where the
lion won't see me."

"Good," said Hornbill. "I'll sit above in my house."

And Python said nothing at all. His head was tucked under his great green coils.

"He's asleep," said Anteater.

The sun went down behind the trees, and the moon came up, round and white.

"The big grass bed looks silver in the moonlight," whispered Anteater.

"Shhhhhh," said Hornbill. "I can see the lion coming through the trees."

The lion was purring and licking his chops. "Ahhhhh! What a breakfast I'll have," he said. "But first I'll find a place to spend the night." He pushed his way through the dark trumpet vines and stood before the bed.

"What's THIS?" he roared. "A big grass bed in the middle of the jungle? I'll try it out for size." He lay down and curled his great tail about him. "Perfect!" he purred. "I'll have a good night's rest." And soon he was fast asleep.

"SQUAWK! SQUAWK! Squawk Squawk Screeeech! Screeeeeech SQUAWK!"

"Good grief!" roared the lion. "What's THAT?"
"It's me, singing," said Hornbill.
"It's the middle of the night!" growled the lion. "QUIET!"

"Thump! Thump! Bump! Bump! Bump! BONG!"

"OUCH!" roared the lion. "WHAT'S GOING ON AROUND HERE?"

"The coconuts are falling off the trees again," said Hornbill. "They always do that at night."

"GOOD HEAVENS!" roared the lion. He turned over and closed his eyes.

Trample   Trample Trample Trample Trample Trample!

"OOOOOOOOOOOO!" howled the lion. "SOMETHING'S TRAMPLING OVER MY BED!"

"Those are just the peccaries," said Hornbill. "They run back and forth all night long."

"Why?" asked the lion.

"You've heard of sleepwalking, haven't you?" said Hornbill. "This is sleeprunning."

"Oh," sighed the lion.

The mango tree began to shake. The vines were swinging
back and forth.

"What's wrong with the trees?" said the lion, holding
his head.

"Those are shaky trees," said Hornbill. "They do that
all the time."

"They *do*?"

The lion turned over and sat up again.
"SOMETHING'S CRAWLING IN MY BED!" he yelled.

"Those are just ants," said Hornbill.
"ANTS?"
"We have millions of ants in this part
of the jungle," yawned Hornbill. "I mean
billions, or is it trillions . . . ?"

The lion growled and closed his eyes.

All at once, something large and heavy fell down from above.

"HELP!" roared the lion. "SOMETHING'S GOT ME! HELP!"

He leaped from the bed.

"I'M GOING BACK WHERE
I CAME FROM!" he roared.
"NO LION WOULD LIVE
IN A PLACE LIKE THIS!"

And he hurried away through the trees.

"HE'S GONE!" shouted the peccaries, running out from the vines.

"HE'S GONE!" cried the monkeys, swinging down to the grass.

"He'll never be back," said Elephant.

"I've got to find my ants all over again," said Anteater, "but it was worth it!"

"HOOORAY!" cried Hornbill. "THE LION'S GONE!" But then he stopped. "What was it that got him last?"

"I don't know," said Anteater.

"Guess who?" said Python, climbing up his vine.

"PYTHON!" cried everyone. "It was you!"

"Of course it was me," said Python. "*That's* what *I* could do."

"Well," said Anteater, "not bad. Not bad at all."

"HOORAY FOR PYTHON!" shouted everyone.
"AND HOORAY!" they cried, "FOR US ALL!"

Anteater rubbed his tired eyes.
"I'm going to sleep," he yawned.

"Goodnight, everybody,"
said Hornbill.
He flew up into his mango tree
and found his leafy bed.
"Goodnight, Hornbill,"

yawned his friends.

"Sleep well."

And they all slept soundly, under the moon, in their peaceful, green-vined jungle.